# J·E·W·E·L·S

Belinda Rochelle

# J·E·W·E·L·S

ILLUSTRATED BY
Cornelius Van Wright
AND Ying-Hwa Hu

Dutton · LODESTAR BOOKS · New York

*Library of Congress Cataloging-in-Publication Data*

Rochelle, Belinda.
Jewels/by Belinda Rochelle; illustrated by Cornelius Van Wright and
Ying-Hwa Hu.—1st ed.
p.  cm.
Summary:  During Lea Mae's annual summer visit her great-grandmother
'Ma dear tells her wonderful stories about their family members and the past,
stories that are jewels of African-American history.
ISBN 0-525-67502-7 (alk. paper)
1. Afro-Americans—Juvenile fiction.  [1. Afro-Americans—Fiction.
2.Great-grandmothers—Fiction.]  I. Van Wright, Cornelius, ill.
II. Hu, Ying-Hwa, ill.  III. Title.  PZ7.R5864Je  1998
[E]—dc20       96-9797   CIP   AC

Published in the United States by Lodestar Books,
an affiliate of Dutton Children's Books,
a member of Penguin Putnam Inc.,
375 Hudson Street, New York, New York  10014

Published simultaneously in Canada
by McClelland & Stewart, Toronto

Editor: Rosemary Brosnan   Designer: Barbara Powderly
Printed in Hong Kong   First Edition   10 9 8 7 6 5 4 3 2 1

to my daughter, Shevon
B.R.

to Wilhemina Holmes
C.V.W. & Y.H.

MY FAVORITE TIME is summer. Every summer my mom and dad take me to stay with 'Ma dear and Pop Henry. To get to their house, Dad drives for hours, chasing the disappearing day. The buildings of the city give way to open fields and tall trees that bend and sway as if to say hello.

Their dogs, Bandit and Buddy, greet us first. They run alongside the car, and when we get out, they smother us with wet, sloppy kisses. When 'Ma dear sees us, her eyes begin to fill with tears.

"Aren't you glad we're here?" I ask.

"Child, these are tears of joy," she says and hugs me close.

'Ma dear and Pop Henry are my great-grandparents. They are my best friends, too. Pop Henry is my mother's grandfather, and 'Ma dear is my mother's grandmother. Mom calls her Grandmother dear, but I call her 'Ma dear, for short. Her real name is Lea Mae; it is my name, too.

At Pop Henry and 'Ma dear's house, neighbors gather every evening to listen to 'Ma dear's stories. Mr. Brown, who owns a small grocery store, is there. He has a big, round belly and a loud, friendly laugh that makes everyone around him laugh, too. Mrs. Wallace, the retired schoolteacher, who wears her eyeglasses at the very tip of her nose, soon joins us. We all settle on the front porch, drinking glass after glass of cold lemonade that looks like sunshine. We shell peas as we wait for 'Ma dear to tell her stories. It is nightfall before she begins.

"You don't live so long and not have a story or two to tell," she says. She rises out of her rocking chair.

"That's what led them to freedom," 'Ma dear says as she points to the brightest star in the sky. "It was a sorrowful time, because all people were not free. My great-grandfather James and his family escaped from slavery and headed North. They were tired and hungry from walking for almost seven days. Their shoes were old and worn, their clothes not warm enough to protect them from the cold. James and his family were lost and frightened. They could hear the search dogs barking, could hear them running through the woods. Right behind them was slavery and maybe even death. James huddled his family close as the dogs got nearer. All of a sudden she appeared—a small woman dressed in men's clothing.

" 'That star will lead you to freedom,' the woman whispered, and she led them through the night, the star their only light. They walked until they came to a house where they would be safe. It was a hiding place on the underground railroad—the beginning of freedom. When they turned around to thank the woman, she was gone. But James knew who it was even though she never uttered her name."

"Who was it, 'Ma dear?" I ask. 'Ma dear looks at me and smiles.

"Child, it was Harriet . . . Harriet Tubman." I gaze up at the sky, and the star sparkles brightly like a beacon.

'Ma dear's best stories are the true stories, her story, my family's story.

"You know, Pop Henry built our first house by himself," she says when the neighbors have gone home and she is tucking me into bed. "Back then we didn't have television; we didn't even have electricity. Our only light was from oil lamps, candles, and sun. Our only heat came from an old woodstove. I gave birth to all of my children in that house, Lea Mae.

"Let me tell you the story of a very special night. My belly was full and round with my second child. Pop Henry had gone to get the midwife, and I was alone. I was so afraid I was going to lose the baby.

My first child, Jericho, had died because the hospital nearby didn't take colored people then, and I rocked that child into the arms of death. I rubbed my belly and told this little one to wait, to hold out until Pop Henry could get back with the midwife. We waited for hours, and finally Pop Henry and the midwife arrived. That's how your grandmother got her name—Patience."

During light rain showers, 'Ma dear and I walk outside
without our shoes. The grass tickles our feet; we slip and slide
and let mud squish between our toes. We catch raindrops with
the tips of our tongues.

At night we punch holes in the lids of mason jars, and I
catch lightning bugs that flicker on and off like green night-
lights. We listen to crickets and bullfrogs and laugh as Bandit
and Buddy bark at the moon.

On other days 'Ma dear just sits in a large, comfortable easy chair next to an open window. She daydreams like I do when I'm at home and I feel all alone. But then 'Ma dear takes a photograph album from the special chest that she keeps locked.

"This here is my grandfather," she says. "Your great-great-great grandfather, six generations back. His name was Harold Jefferson. He was a member of the Buffalo soldiers, brave colored men who fought in the Civil War. After the war the Buffalo soldiers went out West and scouted the land. They built new roads and protected the mail coaches and settlers."

She points to another very special photograph. It is a picture of 'Ma dear perched on top of a piano. She is smiling at the two men who stand next to her holding her hands.

"This is the Count and the Duke, the royalty of jazz," she says. 'Ma dear has always loved music.

Sometimes 'Ma dear plays records by Bessie Smith, Count Basie, and Duke Ellington. 'Ma dear taught my mother the words, and my mother taught me. 'Ma dear lets me wear a flapper dress, high, high heel shoes, and necklaces of bright beads that swing from my neck.

"Come on, Miss Lea, I want to tell you the story of the night I met the Count and the Duke. It was my first visit to New York City," 'Ma dear says. "Let me introduce you to the Count, Count Basie that is: 'Count, this is my great-granddaughter, Miss Lea.' And let me introduce you to the Duke: 'Duke Ellington, meet my great-granddaughter, Miss Lea.'"

I bow my head and curtsy. 'Ma dear moves her head from side to side. Tapping our feet, we hum and sing. Then she grabs my hands, and we dance. Pop Henry joins us. He pulls 'Ma dear into his arms, and they dance cheek to cheek, whirling around the room. Pop Henry leans his head back and laughs, and so do I.

Sundays are very special days. 'Ma dear puts on fancy clothes and an elegant hat. Pop Henry wears a suit, and I wear my best pink dress, with the bow in the back. As we walk to Shiloh Baptist Church, Pop Henry and I tug at our collars. 'Ma dear points her finger and shakes her head to scold us. On Sundays you don't need a watch to tell the time: Church bells ring every hour. People gather from all around wearing their Sunday best. The choir sings, and we all clap our hands as 'Ma dear taps a tambourine.

Every morning Pop Henry and I take long walks. We walk past Fisherman's Pond and throw pebbles that plop and skip across the water. We visit Mr. Brown's store to buy hard rock candy and caramel-covered apples. On the way home, we sit and rest under Brother Matthew, a large oak tree so old and so tall that Pop Henry gave it a name. I climb onto the swing that hangs from Brother Matthew, and Pop Henry pushes me until I can almost touch the clear, bright, blue sky.

Pop Henry brings 'Ma dear peppermints from Mr. Brown's store and wild sunflowers that he has picked from the yard. Time has whitened his hair. I love to plant kisses on his cheeks and rub his curly white whiskers. The smell of his skin is sweet like chocolate. A smile tugs at his lips as if he knows something that you don't. His voice is soft. He always talks about the Jordan River, of crossing over to the land of milk and honey.

"You know, Lea, I have fought in wars. I worked picking tobacco in the fields right here in North Carolina. I have seen so many bad things, seen men beaten with whips, and seen burning crosses in the yards of decent people, all because they were colored. But the secret of life is not to be bitter. I have life still," he says.

My great-grandpa loves little things, things that he can hold in his hands. During the day he sits on the front steps and whittles small scraps of wood. Almost like magic the scraps become tiny elephants, lions, bears, and even little people.

The days pass quickly, and my summer vacation will soon be over. 'Ma dear and I sit on the porch and watch the sunset.

"You know, Lea, you and I are Africa's daughters." She points to the sun. "My father told me once that Africa's daughters are the children of the sun; the sun has touched us. Our darkness is proof of its blessings."

I lay my head in her lap, and she twists my hair into two long braids, then wraps the braids into a crown at the top of my head. Soon I will return home, but this feels like home, too.

"One day I'm going to write down all of the stories. I'm going to be able to tell a story just like you," I whisper. "I promise to save every one of them, so I can remember—and so my children can remember."

'Ma dear smiles. "With each tongue, with each telling, the stories are saved." As proof, she opens my mouth, and word for word, I remember: Like diamonds, sapphires, and rubies, the stories are like jewels to treasure forever.